Hans Christian Andersen's
The Flea and the Professor

A Musical Adaptation by Jordan Harrison

Music by Richard Gray

Lyrics by Jordan Harrison and Richard Gray

A SAMUEL FRENCH ACTING EDITION

SAMUEL FRENCH

FOUNDED 1830

SAMUELFRENCH.COM

HANS CHRISTIAN ANDERSEN'S THE FLEA AND THE PROFESSOR was originally commissioned and produced by Arden Theatre Company in Philadelphia, Pennsylvania on May 4, 2011. The production was directed by Anne Kauffman, with music direction by Dan Kazemi. The Costume Designer was Olivera Gajic and the Lighting Designer was Thom Weaver. Scenic design was by Louisa Thompson, with sound design by Rob Kaplowitz. The Choreographer was Jenn Rose. The Stage Manager was Alec E. Ferrell. The cast was as follows:

THE FLEA . . . . Scott Greer
THE PROFESSOR . . . . Robert McClure
THE CANNIBAL PRINCESS . . . . .Alex Keiper
THE CANNIBAL KING /
HANS CHRISTIAN ANDERSEN. . . . . Kim Sullivan
THE CANNIBAL QUEEN. . . . . .Mary Martello
THE SEA CAPTAIN / LOYAL SUBJECT . . . . .Aaron Cromie
THE STORYTELLER. . . . . Annie McNamara

Developed in the 2012 New Visions Festival at the Kennedy Center
Producing Artistic Director: Terrence J. Nolen,
Managing Director: Amy L. Murphy

CHARACTERS

THE FLEA - Played by a big man.

THE PROFESSOR - Played by a little man.

THE CANNIBAL PRINCESS - Played by a woman of any size. Big voice.

THE CANNIBAL KING - Her father. Later he plays **HANS CHRISTIAN ANDERSEN**

THE CANNIBAL QUEEN - Her mother.

THE SEA CAPTAIN - Also plays **THE LOYAL SUBJECT**

THE STORYTELLER - Whose real name is Livia.

AUTHOR'S NOTES

I imagine that the Flea looks a bit unkempt, à la John Belushi, but speaks in sonorous, dignified tones, à la John Barrymore. The Professor has a bit of Buster Keaton in him. Long, sad face, comically serious.

The Storyteller is a sensible, both-feet-on-the-ground type of woman who didn't grow up dreaming of the limelight. (She probably thought she would be a field journalist instead, like Christiane Amanpour.) She isn't much for pixie dust and poetry, but she takes her job seriously and she's good at it.

Very important: The Cannibals should not be depicted as a 19th-century European's idea of natives. I think of them instead as a brash, nouveau-riche suburban California family with all the comforts money can buy. With a few strange twists to suggest that they are from some civilization heretofore out of contact with ours: Maybe they wear their clothes backwards, maybe they drink with their noses.

The actors playing the Cannibals should not all be of the same race. Also, these secondary characters do some double duty, playing AUDIENCE MEMBERS, FRIENDS, and SAILORS as needed.

MUSICAL NUMBERS

"The Little Big Top" . . . . **PROFESSOR, STORYTELLER**

"The Little Big Top (Reprise)" . . . . **PROFESSOR, FLEA**

"Up Up Up" . . . .**PROFESSOR, FLEA, STORYTELLER, SEA CAPTAIN**

"The Recipe Song". . . . . **CANNIBAL KING, CANNIBAL QUEEN,
PRINCESS, LOYAL SUBJECT**

"Just a Guy" . . . . **PRINCESS, FLEA**

"Gobble" . . . .**ALL**

"Coronation Song" . . . . . **CANNIBAL KING, CANNIBAL QUEEN, PRINCESS,
LOYAL SUBJECT, FLEA**

"Think Thin". . . . .**ALL**

"The Grand Finale" . . . .**ALL**

I. IN WHICH THE PROFESSOR BECOMES THE PROFESSOR.

(We are in a theater, of course. This particular theater has the feeling of a circus. A 19th century circus. There are peanut shells on the ground. The air smells like burnt sugar and animals.)

(Before the show starts, the actors push three mysterious trunks onstage. Battered, old-fashioned traveler's trunks. Just about everything needed for the show should come out of these. [One of the trunks should sit over a trap door, so it can carry rather a lot of things.])

(In the dark, someone blows a whistle. A spotlight finds the **STORYTELLER***, whistle in her mouth.)*

STORYTELLER. Ladies and Gentlemen,

Boys and Girls,

Flora and Fauna,

I give you:

The tale of the Flea and the Professor.

(She opens a trunk. We hear music-box music coming from it.)

(A miniature hot-air balloon rises out of the trunk, manipulated by the **STORYTELLER***. We can see two tiny figures in its basket.)*

STORYTELLER. There was once a hot-air balloonist, and things went badly for him.

(A clap of thunder. The balloon swings wildly.)

A storm tossed his balloon this way and that. But instead of crashing, the balloon kept rising higher and higher, until it seemed he would never get back to earth.

STORYTELLER. *(cont.)* He had just enough time to put his little son in a parachute before he disappeared beyond the clouds forever.

(Lights out on the balloon and up on a life-sized man in a parachute, hanging in the sky. This is the **PROFESSOR.***)*

PROFESSOR. *(searching the sky)* Oh father. My poor father. We might have shared the parachute.

STORYTELLER. This is the Professor. He was just a boy with untied shoelaces then. But, since his name is in the title of the play, you can imagine that he will be very fancy someday.

PROFESSOR. I am not the Professor yet, but I will be someday.

STORYTELLER. And since I'm the one telling the story we don't have to wait: Someday is here!

(She unhooks him from the parachute and he crashes to the ground.)

PROFESSOR. All I want to do is stare at the sky.
All I want is to get back up to the sky where my father is.

(The **STORYTELLER** *pulls him up on his feet, dusts him off.)*

STORYTELLER. But he had to start making his own way in the world.
Up until that point, he had always been provided for, so he didn't have many useful skills. But he practiced all the card tricks his father had taught him, and magic tricks, and throwing his voice.

(The **PROFESSOR** *speaks into his cupped hands.)*

PROFESSOR. Hello in there!

(He pretends to pitch his voice at one of the trunks. The **STORYTELLER** *opens the trunk and it says...)*

PROFESSOR'S VOICE. Hello out there!
My, aren't you a fine fellow.

STORYTELLER. It was true.
For as soon as the Professor grew a mustache and bought some new clothes…

(**TWO ACTORS** *come out and slap a mustache on the* **PROFESSOR***'s face and a top hat on his head.*)

…he could have been mistaken for a respectable gentleman. So people took to calling him the Professor.

ACTOR WITH THE HAT. Good day, Professor.

PROFESSOR. Hullo there.

ACTOR WITH MOUSTACHE. Top of the morning, Professor.

STORYTELLER. No one knew his real name, including me – Which is strange because I was married to him.

(*Light shifts. The* **PROFESSOR** *kneels and offers the* **STORYTELLER** *an enormous diamond ring in a box.*)

PROFESSOR. Be mine, sweet Livia.
Sweet Livia, be mine.

STORYTELLER. *(out)* How do you think I know so much about him?
(*The* **PROFESSOR** *puts the ring on her finger.*)

PROFESSOR. We will perform together and I will cut you in half and shoot you from a cannon! Doesn't that sound nice?

STORYTELLER. *(to the* **PROFESSOR** *now)* I hear it's a difficult life, acting on the legitimate stage.

PROFESSOR. But this won't be anywhere near legitimate! Besides, it isn't forever. One day we'll save enough money to get a hot-air balloon and travel the sky.

STORYTELLER. I'm fine here on the ground.

PROFESSOR. But wait 'til you see it up there!

STORYTELLER. Why are you always looking up at the sky?
(*Short pause. Then, gently:*) He's not coming back – you know that, don't you?

PROFESSOR. I know. It's just that it used to be home. I thought it could be our home too.

STORYTELLER. *(out again)* For a time, it seemed like a nice idea. Saving up for the sky.

(The **OTHER ACTORS** *sit in the front row, as 19th century audience members. One of them uses opera glasses, even though he's just a few feet from the action. Another unwraps a hard candy, loudly.)*

PROFESSOR. Drum roll, please.

(A drum roll obliges.)

Ladies and Gentlemen,

May I present, the luminous Livia!

(The **PROFESSOR** *tears away her plain suit and the* **STORYTELLER** *is wearing a spangled magician's-assistant outfit underneath.)*

STORYTELLER. I hate this thing. I feel like a Christmas ornament.

PROFESSOR. Come Livia, it's time for the opening number.

(He starts to sing…)

(SONG: THE LITTLE BIG TOP)

WE ARE NOT THE GREATEST SHOW ON EARTH
WE ARE NOT, AND WE'LL NEVER, EVER BE
WE ARE NOT UNDER THE BIGGEST BIG TOP
AND HERE ARE ALL THE THINGS YOU WILL NOT SEE:
AN ELEPHANT,
AND A KNIFE THROWER,
A STRONG MAN AND HIS BEARDED WIFE.
NO TUMBLERS A-FLYIN',
NO LION OR A LION TAMER
NO HIGH DIVER RISKING LIMB AND LIFE.
WE HAVE NO CAR OF CLOWNS,
NO STAR (OF COURSE),
NO FANCY LADY STANDING ON A FANCY HORSE;
NO JUGGLING SEAL,
NO DANCING COW

WE GOT ABSOLUTELY NOTHING THAT'LL MAKE YOU SAY
    "WOW!"

WE ARE NOT THE GREATEST SHOW ON EARTH
WE ARE NOT, AND WE'LL NEVER, EVER BE –

STORYTELLER. Professor?

PROFESSOR.
WE ARE NOT UNDER THE BIGGEST –

STORYTELLER. Professor! Can I talk to you for a moment?

(The **STORYTELLER** *pulls him aside. They face upstage.)*

(stage whisper) Stop telling them what they're *missing.*
Remember how we agreed to emphasize what we *do*
have?

PROFESSOR. Oh yes.

(The **PROFESSOR** *turns back to us. Then back to*
STORYTELLER.*)*

This is rather awkward.

(The **STORYTELLER** *makes a supportive "Carry on"
gesture. The* **PROFESSOR** *takes up the song again.)*

WE ARE NOT THE GREATEST SHOW ON EARTH –

STORYTELLER.
BUT WE'VE GOT A FEW TRICKS UP OUR SLEEVE!

PROFESSOR & **STORYTELLER.**
WE ARE NOT UNDER THE BIGGEST BIG TOP –
BUT WHEN YOU SEE OUR ACT AT LEAST YOU WILL NOT
    LEAVE!
(spoken to audience, desperate:) Right?

PROFESSOR.
WE'LL MAKE YOU LAUGH (OR AT LEAST GIGGLE)
OUR PEANUTS? THEY TASTE AS GOOD AS MOST.
OUR SECRET'S DRY-ROASTING AND TOASTING
AND SOME FRESH BUTTER
MAKES 'EM BETTER
BUT WE DO NOT LIKE TO BOAST.

(The **STORYTELLER** *walks a very low high-wire.)*

STORYTELLER.
> ON WEEKDAY SHOWS I WALK THE WIRE
> I'M SOMEWHAT PRONE TO NOSEBLEEDS
> SO I CAN'T GET HIGHER.
> ON SATURDAY NIGHTS, I GET ON THE TRAPEZE
> (I WOULD DO IT MUCH MORE OFTEN
> BUT IT'S BAD FOR THE KNEES.)
> *(She falls off the wire, into the* **PROFESSOR***'s arms.)*

PROFESSOR & **STORYTELLER.**
> WE ARE NOT THE GREATEST SHOW ON EARTH
>
> *(short little dance break)*
>
> WE ARE NOT UNDER THE BIGGEST BIG TOP
>
> *(wind-up to the Big Finish)*
>
> WE ARE NOT THE GREATEST SHOW ON EARTH
> WE ARE NOT, AND WE'LL NEVER, EVER BE
> WE ARE NOT UNDER THE BIGGEST BIG TOP
> BUT WE DO THINGS ADEQUATELYYYY!
> *(spoken:)* We're average!

AUDIENCE MEMBERS. Boo!

STORYTELLER. *(out)* The crowds could be hard to please.

(The **AUDIENCE MEMBERS** *throw tomatoes at them.)*

AUDIENCE MEMBERS. Boo! Boo!

STORYTELLER. Why do they throw tomatoes instead of roses?

PROFESSOR. Because roses have thorns. They don't want to prick us.

AUDIENCE MEMBERS. Boo! Boo!

STORYTELLER. Why do they yell, "Boo"?

PROFESSOR. That sounds like, "Woo".

AUDIENCE MEMBERS. Boo!

PROFESSOR. "Woo". They're *wooing* us!

STORYTELLER. My darling, I don't believe you.

PROFESSOR. Just you wait.
We will win them over yet with our greatest illusion, the Disappearing Act!

STORYTELLER. Now because you're such a special audience, I'm going to break the oldest rule in all of magic: *(conspiratorial:)* I'm going to tell you how we did the Disappearing Act.
So everybody lean in close.
Closer.

PROFESSOR. Livia, stop talking to the audience and help me with the act!

STORYTELLER. *(faux innocent)* Coming, Darling.

(We see the following as she describes it.)

First, I'd climb into one of the Professor's trunks. It was just big enough for me. And inside there was a fake back…

(She is out of sight now. We hear her voice amplified.)

So as far as the audience was concerned, I was invisible.

AUDIENCE MEMBER 1. How do they do that?

AUDIENCE MEMBER 2. It's a two-bit trick!

AUDIENCE MEMBER 3. It's smoke and mirrors!

STORYTELLER. *(voice only)* When the Professor opened the suitcase again, I would pop right out.

PROFESSOR. Ta-da!

*(The **PROFESSOR** realizes that she isn't there.)*

STORYTELLER. *(voice only)* Only one evening, when he opened the trunk, I was still invisible. Even to him.

PROFESSOR. Just a minute, ladies and gentlemen.
Technical difficulties.

*(The **PROFESSOR** opens and closes the box several times. Rising desperation.)*

STORYTELLER. *(voice only)* I wasn't inside the trunk, nor was I out. I was not in the whole theater. And I never came back, which really was an impressive trick.

(The **PROFESSOR** *picks up the box and looks under it.)*

PROFESSOR. Livia? *(truly distressed)* Livia!

AUDIENCE MEMBER 4. *(loudly whispering to Audience Member 2)* I didn't know he was this *good.*

AUDIENCE MEMBER 3. Shhh!

PROFESSOR. Livia? Livia, my darling!

(The formerly skeptical **AUDIENCE** *applauds heartily.)*

STORYTELLER'S VOICE. For once, the audience loved it.

(The **AUDIENCE MEMBERS** *throw roses at the* **PROFESSOR**'s *feet.)*

AUDIENCE MEMBERS. Encore! Encore!

STORYTELLER'S VOICE. …But there was nothing left to do as an encore.

II. THE PROFESSOR LOSES EVERYTHING
BUT A FLEA.

(The **STORYTELLER** *reappears to us in another part of the stage, wearing a plain suit again.)*

STORYTELLER. Why did I leave? I loved my husband, but show business was simply too hard.
It wasn't just the tomatoes. There was also scrubbing the sticky floors after the guests went home and before the roaches came. But mostly it was the tomatoes.
After I left, the Professor was very sad.

(The **PROFESSOR** *blows the whistle, half-heartedly. A spotlight finds him.)*

It seemed like half of him was missing. Half of his act, anyway.

(drum roll)

PROFESSOR. Ladies and Gentlemen,
May I present…nobody.

STORYTELLER. Instead of pulling a rabbit out of his hat, he pulled out half a rabbit.

(The **PROFESSOR** *reaches into his hat and pulls out the top half of a plush bunny.)*

PROFESSOR. Ta-da.

STORYTELLER. He only told half of his jokes…

PROFESSOR. Why did the chicken cross the road? *(pause)* That's it. You can all go home now.

STORYTELLER. When the Professor's friends saw how sad he was, they tried tickling him, which is how you get people to laugh when they don't feel like laughing.

(The **FRIENDS** *come out and tickle the* **PROFESSOR.***)*

They tickled him and
Tickled him and
Tickled him and
Tickled him…

(Short pause. Then even more aggressively:)

STORYTELLER. *(cont.)* And tickled him and
Tickled him and
Tickled him!
But even then, he just couldn't laugh. So his friends
gave up.

(The **FRIENDS** *scatter, taking pieces of the act with them.)*

People stopped coming to see his act. The Professor
had to pawn all his magic tricks, and his clothes became
worn and shabby.

(One **FRIEND** *tears one of his sleeves off on the way out.
Another* **FRIEND** *rips off his moustache.)*

PROFESSOR. Hey!

STORYTELLER. Even the hat on his head.

(While the **PROFESSOR** *is distracted, the third* **FRIEND**
*punches a hole through his top hat and puts it back on
his head. The* **PROFESSOR** *is alone now.)*

STORYTELLER. Soon the Professor had nothing left in the
whole world but a single flea who lived in his waistcoat.

PROFESSOR. Ouch!

VOICE OF THE FLEA. Sorry.

PROFESSOR. *(looking around)* Who's there?

VOICE OF THE FLEA. In here.

(The **PROFESSOR** *reaches into his waistcoat, then peers
into his seemingly empty hand.)*

STORYTELLER. There was nothing in the Professor's hand
but a single red speck, like a piece of paprika.

PROFESSOR. Hello?

(A very robust voice comes from the **PROFESSOR** *'s hand.)*

VOICE OF THE FLEA. Hi there.

PROFESSOR. Who are you?

VOICE OF THE FLEA. My name's Herman. I'm your flea.

PROFESSOR. Ouch!

VOICE OF THE FLEA. Sorry. Sometimes I can't help myself. You see, biting is in my nature.

STORYTELLER. It was the Flea's nature to sink his teeth into someone and never let go.

The fancy scientists call this parasitism, but we can just call it biting.

(The **STORYTELLER** *disappears into shadows.)*

And since everyone else the Professor had ever known had left him, it was a nice change of pace – someone who would hold on and never let go.

PROFESSOR. *(looking into his palm)* Herman?

VOICE OF THE FLEA. Right here.

PROFESSOR. I've lost my act. I've lost my lovely assistant.

I don't suppose, can *you* do any tricks?

VOICE OF THE FLEA. What are tricks?

PROFESSOR. Like wiggling your ears,

Or rolling your tongue,

Or patting your head and rubbing your tummy at the same time.

VOICE OF THE FLEA. I can jump.

PROFESSOR. Anyone can jump.

VOICE OF THE FLEA. No, I mean, I can *jump.*

(The **STORYTELLER** *reappears in another part of the space.)*

STORYTELLER. And with that, the Flea jumped high in the air and turned twenty-two somersaults before landing gently on his feet.

PROFESSOR. *(looking up in the rafters, open-mouthed)* Wow.

You are coming back down, aren't you?

VOICE OF THE FLEA. I am back down. I'm sitting on your shoulder.

PROFESSOR. Ah, there you are.

VOICE OF THE FLEA. No, the other shoulder.

PROFESSOR. Ah.

VOICE OF THE FLEA. Now I'm sitting on your wrist.

PROFESSOR. Ah.

VOICE OF THE FLEA. Other wrist.

STORYTELLER. As incredible as this all was, it would be annoying to watch a play about someone you can't see.

(The actors come out with a giant magnifying glass. They hold it in front of the **PROFESSOR***'s hand.)*

So I asked around, and we found a very powerful magnifying glass in the basement of the theater. Ladies and Gentlemen, for your viewing pleasure, may I present…

Herman the Flea!

(The **FLEA***, now played by an actor in a big red flea suit, comes leaping through the magnifying glass. He turns a somersault before coming to a not-so-gentle landing.)*

FLEA. Ow, my back.

PROFESSOR. Are you okay?

FLEA. Fine, fine. Did you know the common flea can leap over two hundred times his own body length?

PROFESSOR. I didn't know!

FLEA. And I am no simple common flea:

I have human blood in me, you see.

STORYTELLER. You might be wondering, how did the Flea come to have human blood in him?

PROFESSOR. How did you come to have human blood in you?

FLEA. It's on my mother's side, I think. My mother's mother's only sister's sister's only daughter's only son was human.

PROFESSOR. You mother's mother's only sister's sister's only daughter's only son?

FLEA. Yes.

PROFESSOR. That's you.

FLEA. No.

PROFESSOR. Yes, you fool.

FLEA. Well that's not right at all. But someone somewhere was part human.

PROFESSOR. I don't think so.

FLEA. It's my family tree.

PROFESSOR. You know what I think?

I think you have human blood in you from biting humans and drinking their blood.

*(The **PROFESSOR** looks down and sees the **FLEA** biting his arm.)*

FLEA. *(with mouthful of arm)* It's a theory.

(light shifts)

STORYTELLER. The Professor got it into his head to train the Flea as his new star performer. It took many months for the Flea to get into shape.

*(light on the **FLEA** doing pushups)*

Every morning, the Professor gave the Flea a tiny thimbleful of his blood for breakfast. Which for fleas is like spinach for Popeye times a hundred.

*(The **FLEA** starts doing the hard kind of pushups, clapping hands in between each pushup.)*

The Professor taught the Flea all kinds of tricks, like getting shot out of a cannon…

(Blackout. Drum roll. Sound of a cannon.)

*(When light returns, the **FLEA** is far across the stage. He has landed on his belly. Canned applause.)*

And diving head first into a bucket of water…

(Blackout. Drum roll. Sound of a splash.)

*(When light returns, the **FLEA** is sitting in a bucket of water. Canned applause. When the **FLEA** stands up, the bucket is still attached to his rump.)*

STORYTELLER. Scariest of all, he learned to say the alphabet backwards…

(Drum roll. The **FLEA** *assumes a pose of great concentration.)*

FLEA. Z, Y, X, W, V, U, T, S, R, Q, Q...
Shoot.

(blackout)

STORYTELLER. Until finally, it was the big day of his debut.

PROFESSOR. Ladies and Gentlemen, Boys and Girls,
He's smaller than a centimeter,
He's mightier than a millipede,
Tonight for the first time, I present...
the Phenomenal Flea!

(The **FLEA** *and the* **PROFESSOR** *sing a triumphant little reprise of the "Little Big Top" song...)*

(*SONG: THE LITTLE BIG TOP (REPRISE)*)

FLEA & PROFESSOR.
WE ARE NOT THE GREATEST SHOW ON EARTH
BUT WHAT WE'VE GOT IS THE NOTION OF SURPRISE.

(The **FLEA** *hides behind the* **PROFESSOR.** *)*

PROFESSOR.
"THERE'S NOTHING THERE," YOU MAY SAY. LOOK CLOSER...

(The **FLEA** *pops out again.)*

FLEA & PROFESSOR.
TO SEE THE BIG RED TALENT RIGHT BEFORE YOUR EYES!
WE ARE NOT THE GREATEST SHOW ON EARTH
WE ARE NOT, BUT SOMEDAY WE HOPE TO BE
WE ARE NOT UNDER THE BIGGEST BIG TOP
BUT WE'RE THE ONLY CIRCUS WITH A FLEA!

(big finish:)

A FLEA!!!

III. IN WHICH THEY TRAVEL
FAR AND ALSO WIDE.

STORYTELLER. And so the very first flea circus was born. The Professor was proud of the Flea, and the Flea was proud of himself.

Wherever they went they were welcomed as heroes.

(The **STORYTELLER** *opens a little door in the side of one of the trunks. She pushes a miniature train out of it, laying track piece by piece. Light rises on the* **FLEA** *and the* **PROFESSOR** *sleeping on the other trunks.)*

They always traveled in the fourth-class cabin, which took them there just as quickly as first-class. First they conquered Paris…

PROFESSOR. *Bonjour, Mes Enfants!*

STORYTELLER. Then Venice…

PROFESSOR. *Buon Giorno, Ragazzi!*

STORYTELLER. Then farthest India…

PROFESSOR. *Namaste bu-chaan.*

STORYTELLER. Whatever city they were in, it made no difference – the Flea conquered them all. Peasants and presidents saw him and gave him high praise. He was now a famous Flea, and everywhere they went, he demanded a velvet robe and green M&M's in his dressing room.

(The actors help the **FLEA** *into a velvet robe.)*

FLEA. This is the life.

PROFESSOR. Just be careful you don't get decadent.

FLEA. *(as one of the actors feeds him a green M&M's)* What's decadent?

PROFESSOR. Decadent is like…a big chocolate cake.

FLEA. So, don't be like a big chocolate cake.

PROFESSOR. Just remember that once we had nothing but each other, and we could just as easily have that again.

FLEA. That wasn't so bad.

PROFESSOR. It wasn't?

FLEA. When all we had was each other, that was still plenty.

PROFESSOR. You know you're very sweet for a flea.

    Ouch!

FLEA. *(with a mouthful of elbow)* Sorry. In my nature.

STORYTELLER. Before long, they had traveled all of the countries in the world together.

    (The **STORYTELLER** *opens a trunk. A miniature tallship rises out, with all its sails unfurled. The* **STORYTELLER** *manipulates it. Another actor might hold a portable fan to suggest the ocean breeze.)*

    All the countries, that is, except one.

SEA CAPTAIN. All aboard for the Cannibal Islands!

FLEA. Where'd he say we're going?

PROFESSOR. It doesn't really matter, as long as there's an audience there.

    (A **SEA CAPTAIN** *with a peg leg holds a steering wheel, attached to nothing. The* **PROFESSOR** *looks at the sky through a telescope.)*

STORYTELLER. They had become quite a pair, the Flea and the Professor. And together, nothing could defeat them.

    (The **FLEA** *leans over the edge, seasick.)*

    Well, almost nothing.

PROFESSOR. You okay?

FLEA. *(re: his stomach)* This is my first time on a ship. And my last.

PROFESSOR. Someday it'll be different…

FLEA. Someday?

PROFESSOR. Someday we'll have a great balloon to fly in.

FLEA. Why a balloon?

PROFESSOR. You know how it feels when you jump way up in the sky?

FLEA. It's the best. It feels like home.

PROFESSOR. Well, I used to feel like that too.

(Music. Together they sing…)

(SONG: UP UP UP)

FLEA & PROFESSOR.
UP, UP, UP IN THE SKY
THAT'S THE ONE PLACE, THE ONE PLACE TO BE
I CAN'T GET THERE MYSELF
BUT PERHAPS WITH A FLEA?

FLEA. I assume you mean me.

PROFESSOR. Uh-huh.
UP, UP, UP IN THE SKY
THAT'S THE ONE PLACE

FLEA.
THAT'S THE ONE PLACE TO BE

PROFESSOR.
THE ONE PLACE TO BE
IN THE CLOUDS, LOOKING DOWN
EVERYONE SMALL AS –

FLEA. A flea?

PROFESSOR.
I WAS GOING TO SAY ANT.

FLEA.
THERE'S NO REASON YOU CAN'T
BUT A FLEA IS MUCH MORE POETICAL
NOT TO MENTION COPACETICAL.

PROFESSOR.
BUT, IF YOU'RE TALKING ALPHABETICAL, THEN
(trailing off) ant would come before flea…

FLEA.	**PROFESSOR.**
UP, UP, UP	
UP IN THE SKY	UP IN THE SKY
THAT'S THE ONE PLACE…	
	THAT'S THE ONE PLACE
THE ONE PLACE FOR ME	FOR ME.
I'VE BEEN STUCK IN A VEST	

FOR A YEAR OR TWO OR
 THREE.

FLEA/PROFESSOR.   **STORYTELLER/SEA CAPTAIN.**

UP, UP, UP IN THE SKY
THAT'S THE ONE PLACE

          THAT'S THE ONE PLACE
TO BE   TO BE
THERE'S A WHOLE LOT OF
 WORLD
WAITING OUT THERE TO   WAITING OUT THERE TO
 SEE.   SEE.
UP IN THE AIR…   UP IN THE AIR

FLEA & PROFESSOR.

NEVER A CARE

PROFESSOR.

NO FOURTH-CLASS SEATS, NO BUMPY STREETS,
NO SMOKE IN YOUR EYES –

FLEA & PROFESSOR.

IT'S THE ONLY KIND OF TRAVEL
FOR TWO FAMOUS GUYS!

STORYTELLER & SEA CAPTAIN.

UP IN THE AIR…

FLEA.

NO TOSS-AND-TURNING, STOMACH-CHURNING
ALL THE ABOVE –

ALL.

IT'S THE ONLY KIND OF TRAVEL –
THE ONLY KIND OF TRAVEL

FLEA & SEA CAPTAIN.

THAT'S FIT FOR A DOVE.

ALL.

UP, UP, UP IN THE SKY

PROFESSOR.

NO HEARTBREAK, NO HEARTACHE,
NO FEELING SO BLUE –
IT'S THE ONE PLACE
WHERE NO ONE CAN WALK OUT ON YOU.

STORYTELLER. At that point, the Flea and the Professor made a pledge to remain bachelors forever.

PROFESSOR. Pinky swear?

FLEA. Pinky swear.

STORYTELLER. And that one day they would travel the sky together, happy and free.

FLEA. Pinky swear?

Professor?

PROFESSOR. *(lost in thought)* Oh yes.

Pinky swear.

STORYTELLER. Just as the Professor vowed never to marry again, he secretly wondered if he could forget Livia that easily. Sometimes he imagined he saw her…

PROFESSOR. *(looking straight at her)* Livia?

(The **STORYTELLER** *ducks into a shadow.)*

FLEA. Come on, forget about her.

(singing again:)

UP, UP, UP IN THE SKY
THAT'S THE ONE PLACE
THE ONE PLACE TO GO
ALL THE TROUBLES OF MAN
SO FAR DOWN BELOW

STORYTELLER & **SEA CAPTAIN**.

UP, UP, UP IN THE SKY

PROFESSOR & FLEA.

UP, UP, UP IN THE SKY
SOMEDAY
WE'LL GO UP, UP, UP, UP, UP, UP, UP
AND AWAY!

PROFESSOR. Where are we, Captain?

SEA CAPTAIN. I'm not sure. I lost the compass. And the sextant. And the GPS.

PROFESSOR. Oh no.

SEA CAPTAIN. But we must be nearing land.

PROFESSOR. How do you know?

(The **SEA CAPTAIN** *holds a plastic seagull aloft.)*

SEA CAPTAIN. See that seagull?

PROFESSOR. Yes.

SEA CAPTAIN. You don't see a gull like that out in the middle of nowhere. He must have come from dry land, or else he's headed there…

FLEA. *(looking in telescope)* Land ahoy!

(The **STORYTELLER** *opens the magic trunk. A full-sized palm tree rises out of it.)*

PROFESSOR. Thank heaven.

STORYTELLER. And so at last they had reached a land where the sand was white-hot

(The **FLEA** *touches his foot to imaginary sand.)*

FLEA. *(hopping on one leg)* Ouch!

STORYTELLER. And the water was blue-cool.

(The **FLEA** *douses his foot in imaginary water, with a "splash" sound.)*

FLEA. Aaaah.

PROFESSOR. Say, have you seen the Captain?

FLEA. That's strange.

PROFESSOR. Oh Captain!

FLEA. My Captain!

(The **PROFESSOR** *spies a stick lying in the sand.)*

PROFESSOR. Hold on. Isn't that his peg leg?

FLEA. Now where would he be going without that?

PROFESSOR. Look – tracks in the sand, heading off this way!

(The **FLEA** *and the* **PROFESSOR** *head off, following the tracks.)*

(continuous into…)

IV. WHAT STRANGE NEW LAND IS THIS.

STORYTELLER. What they didn't know yet, but I know because I'm the Storyteller,
was that this island was the domain of...

(The **LOYAL SUBJECT** *appears and plays a trumpet flourish.)*

CANNIBAL KING. The Cannibal King!

(a more elaborate trumpet flourish)

CANNIBAL QUEEN. And the Cannibal Queen!

STORYTELLER. But the true leader of the land turned out to be...

(a still more elaborate flourish)

PRINCESS. The Cannibal Princess!

(The trumpet finishes with a little riff.)

PRINCESS. This is just the spot for our Cannibal picnic.

CANNIBAL QUEEN. But the sand is even softer over here, my treasure.

PRINCESS. I said I want the picnic *here!*

STORYTELLER. The Princess was only twelve years old, but she ruled this strange land just the same.
Now, it is quite unusual for children in fairy tales to have two parents. Parents seem to die an awful lot in fairy tales, you may have noticed. There was Snow White's mother, and Bambi's mother, and of course, the Professor's poor father (and we can only assume his mother, unless he just never introduced me to her).
Long story short, being a character in a fairy tale, the Princess was very lucky that both her parents were around.

PRINCESS. *(not feeling lucky)* I am so lucky.

STORYTELLER. She was very lucky to have two parents to tell her:

CANNIBAL QUEEN. Don't pout too much or you'll give yourself a mouth-ache.

(The **PRINCESS** *scrunches up her nose.)*

STORYTELLER. And to tell her:

CANNIBAL KING. Don't scrunch up your nose or you'll give yourself a nose-ache.

STORYTELLER. All in all, she was a very lucky Princess.

PRINCESS. I am so lucky.

STORYTELLER. But although she had never been cold or hungry in her life, something had gone quite wrong with her manners. For you see, the Princess was just as beautiful as she was rude.

PRINCESS. *(addressing the palm tree)* What're you looking at, palm tree!

STORYTELLER. …Which is to say, she was very beautiful indeed.

PRINCESS. Get out of my toes, sand! I'm tired of you! I'm tired of everything on this stupid island!

STORYTELLER. In the land of the Cannibals, everyone wore a single bone on the top of their head. Why did they do this?

CANNIBAL QUEEN. Because it would be immodest to wear *two* bones.

STORYTELLER. But only the Princess was allowed to carry a pretty pink flamingo feather fan.

(The **PRINCESS** *opens her fan and fans herself with it. It fairly shimmers.)*

LOYAL SUBJECT. Your pretty pink flamingo feather fan is most becoming, Your Highness.

PRINCESS. Say that ten times fast, for my amusement!

LOYAL SUBJECT. Pretty pink flamingo feather fan
Pretty pink flamingo feather fan
Pretty pink flamingo feather fan
Pretty pink flamingo –

PRINCESS. That's enough. I'm already bored.

STORYTELLER. Because of the way she acted, it was easy to forget that the Princess was beautiful.

(The **PRINCESS** *blows her nose with the* **STORYTELLER***'s shirt.)*

STORYTELLER. *(cont.)* Yes, um, thank you for that.

Now let me see – there was one more thing I was supposed to tell you about the Cannibals.

(Unseen by the **STORYTELLER***, the* **CANNIBAL KING** *and* **CANNIBAL QUEEN** *push on an enormous cauldron.)*

One very important thing…

What could it be…

(she sees it now) Ah yes. The Cannibals liked to eat people.

(The **CANNIBALS** *gather round the cauldron and sing…)*

*(**SONG: THE RECIPE SONG**)*

CANNIBALS.

THIS IS A RECIPE
AN ANCIENT FAMILY RECIPE,
FOR SLOW COOKED FANCY HUMAN -
A PRETTY TASTY STEW, MAN.
SERVED HOT OR COLD, IT'S OUT OF SIGHT

CANNIBAL QUEEN.

IT'S HEAVEN IF YOU MAKE IT RIGHT

CANNIBALS.

A RECIPE
AN ANCIENT FAMILY RECIPE
FOR SLOW COOKED

LOYAL SUBJECT. Free Range!

CANNIBALS.

HUMAN
OUR FAVORITE THING TO CHEW, MAN.
NO NEED FOR SIDES OR SPECIAL SAUCE

CANNIBAL KING. *(in a basso voice)*
JUST DON'T FORGET THE DENTAL FLOSS.

CANNIBALS.
THIS IS A RECIPE
A MOST DELICIOUS RECIPE
NO MATTER HOW YOU SKIN IT.
HERE IS WHAT IS IN IT:

CANNIBAL QUEEN.
ONE BIG CAULDRON

PRINCESS.
WATER FROM THE CREEK-A

LOYAL SUBJECT.
A PINCH OF PEPPER

CANNIBAL KING.
A PINCH OF SALT

CANNIBAL QUEEN.
A PINCH OF PAPRIKA

PRINCESS. *(with sinister glee)* One human.

CANNIBALS.
EUREKA!
YOU BOIL IT ALL FOR TWENTY HOURS
AND THEN FOUR MORE
TO SAVOR ALL THE FLAVOR THAT'LL
COME TO THE FORE
THAT'S IT
THAT'S ALL YOU NEED
TO MAKE SLOW-COOKED FANCY HUMAN!

(touching the bones on their heads)

BONE…APPETIT!

(They tuck the edge of a checkered tablecloth into their shirts, like a bib.)

STORYTELLER. The song was so catchy that they sang it before every meal. But in fact, the Cannibals didn't cook human every day.

CANNIBAL QUEEN. That would be just decadent.

STORYTELLER. (Have you ever noticed how, once you learn a new word, it comes up all the time?)

(*The* **CANNIBALS** *look at her, impatient.*)

Sorry – where was I.
Oh yes, the Cannibals didn't eat human every day. That's a common misconception about Cannibals.

(*The* **CANNIBAL QUEEN** *reaches into the cauldron with a big wooden spoon.*)

CANNIBAL QUEEN. Pasta salad, coming right up!

PRINCESS. But I want to eat human *now!*

CANNIBAL KING. Patience, my treasure –
We're saving the Sea Captain for the big occasion tomorrow.

STORYTELLER. *(stage whisper)* The big occasion was Cannibalia, the biggest party of the year.

PRINCESS. *(to audience, menacing)* And you better hope you're not invited!

CANNIBAL QUEEN. Besides, the Captain looks a little stringy. That'll give us time to fatten him up.

CANNIBAL KING. Too bad he's so old. Shoulder of child with pepper sauce is the most delicate.

CANNIBAL QUEEN. At least he won't need any extra salt – all those years marinating in the sea air…

CANNIBAL KING. More pasta please.

CANNIBAL QUEEN. You like it?

CANNIBAL KING. *(affirmative, with a mouthful)* Mmmph.

PRINCESS. *(playing with her food)* It could use more human. And by that I mean *any* human.

(*The* **CANNIBALS** *finish their meal in five seconds flat, wipe their mouths with the tablecloth, and toss the plates aside. They lie on their backs in the sand, patting their full tummies.*)

STORYTELLER. Now, if you're a smarty-pants, you may be wondering how Cannibals on a desert island speak perfect English. The answer is: they don't. (*She pats a* *big metal switch on the wall.)* But with this nifty Cannibal Translator, we can understand every word. *(She turns the switch to the "off" position.)* We can understand that when they say…

CANNIBAL QUEEN. Gobble gobble gobble gobble?

PRINCESS. Gobble.

(The **STORYTELLER** *turns the switch back to "on.")*

STORYTELLER. …what they're really saying is:

CANNIBAL QUEEN. *(enticing the* **PRINCESS***)* Who wants to go beachcombing?

PRINCESS. *Borrr-*ing.

STORYTELLER. Or:

CANNIBAL KING. Who wants to go bodysurfing?

PRINCESS. *Borrr-*ing.

STORYTELLER. This was no way for a princess to talk to her mother and father.

CANNIBAL QUEEN. *(to the* **CANNIBAL KING**, *as they leave)* What is wrong with that child.

STORYTELLER. Even a Cannibal princess.

PRINCESS. *(to* **LOYAL SUBJECT***)* I think I'll bury you in the sand instead.

LOYAL SUBJECT. I would be honored, Your Majesty.

PRINCESS. I think today I'll bury you head-first.

LOYAL SUBJECT. Yes, your Royal Heinousness.

(He follows the **PRINCESS** *off.)*

(continuous into…)

V. THE PRINCESS AND THE FLEA.

(The second they're gone, the **PROFESSOR** *comes on from the other direction, rather overdressed in a safari outfit. Khaki shorts, helmet, binoculars. The* **FLEA** *trails behind.)*

STORYTELLER. Meanwhile, the Professor and the Flea were having a wonderful time exploring the island.

FLEA. *(delirious with thirst)* Water…
Water…

STORYTELLER. …But they had yet to encounter any signs of human civilization.

PROFESSOR. Amazing – there seems to be very little hunger on this island. The juicy juicy coconuts fall right from the tree into your lap.

(A coconut falls from the tree in front of them.)

The flying fish jump out of the water and into your frying pan.

(Someone throws a rubber fish across the stage. The **PROFESSOR** *catches it with a frying pan.)*

It's a very sound ecosystem. The black widow spiders eat the tse-tse flies. The diseased rats eat the black widow spiders. The wild hogs smash the diseased rats underfoot. The apes catch the wild hogs and baste them in a sort of primitive barbecue sauce. Very sound indeed.

(The **PROFESSOR** *sees the cauldron.)*

Herman?

FLEA. *(drinking from the coconut with a bendy straw)* You should really try this.

PROFESSOR. Look over there. Do you know what this means?

FLEA. No.

PROFESSOR. It's the first sign of civilization. The island is populated after all! *(sudden change of tone)* I only hope this isn't the part of the world where they eat honorable men.

FLEA. Well, you're not very honorable, and I'm not much of a man. So I wouldn't worry.

PROFESSOR. What do you think is *in* that suspicious, man-sized cauldron.

FLEA. It looks like pasta salad.

PROFESSOR. A society of vegetarian natives!

(*The* **PRINCESS** *mopes her way onto the stage, kicking sand and humming the Recipe Song.*)

Then it turns out we have no reason to fear…
(*Jinxingly:*) No reason whatsoever.

PRINCESS. Who are you.

PROFESSOR. Oh. Hello Little Girl.

I'm the Professor.

PRINCESS. Funny, you don't *look* very smart.

STORYTELLER. The Professor didn't really know how to talk to children.

PROFESSOR. (*patronizing*) Do you know where your mummy and daddy are?

PRINCESS. Do you know where *your* mummy and daddy are?

PROFESSOR. (*She's hit a nerve.*) No.

STORYTELLER. The trouble was, the Professor didn't really *know* any children.

He thought it was different than talking to adults.

PROFESSOR. So, how do things look from down there?

(*The* **PRINCESS** *sniffs the air.*)

PRINCESS. You smell like a human. And I eat humans for DINNER.

STORYTELLER. Luckily, just then, the Flea landed on the Princess's shoulder…

PRINCESS. Ouch!

FLEA. Sorry.

STORYTELLER. …And it was love at first bite. *(to herself:)* Sometimes I am so *good.*

*(The **FLEA** and the **PRINCESS** look at each other for the first time. We hear sweet, orchestral music.)*

STORYTELLER. This was one of those moments in life when all you can do is sing.

*(The **PRINCESS** sings a soaring little love song. Soon the **FLEA** joins in. Caught in the middle, the **PROFESSOR** doesn't know what to do with himself.)*

*(**SONG: JUST A GUY**)*

PRINCESS.
> HE'S JUST A GUY
> WHO HAPPENS TO BE A FLEA
> HE'S JUST A GUY
> WHO HAPPENS TO MAKE MY HEART SING
> AND I'M JUST A GIRL
> WHO YELLS AND SCREAMS
> BUT MUST'VE HARBORED DREAMS
> OF YOU AND ME –
> ME AND FLEA!

PRINCESS.
> HE'S JUST A GUY
> WHO HAPPENS TO BE A
> > FLEA

FLEA.
> I HAPPEN TO BE A FLEA,
> IT'S TRUE

PRINCESS.
> HE'S JUST A GUY
> WHO'S A LOVELY SHADE
> > OF RED

FLEA.
> I'M A LOVELY SHADE OF
> > RED,
> BUT I DON'T LET IT GO TO
> > MY HEAD!

PRINCESS.
> AND I'M JUST A GIRL
> WHO HAD NO HEART
> 'TIL HE SAT IN MY HAND

AND I FELL APART.
I LOVE MY FLY –

FLEA. Flea.

PRINCESS. Right.

HE'S JUST A GUY.

FLEA.

I'M JUST A FLEA
WHO HAPPENS TO BE A
GUY...

PRINCESS.

COULD IT BE I'D FALL
FOR SOMETHING SO
SMALL?

A FLEA

SO RED?

WHO INSTEAD
WANTS TO EXPLORE

PERHAPS HE'S MORE
THAN JUST A GUY

NOT JUST A GIRL

NOT JUST A MITE

A FLEA –

ALL RIGHT,

I'LL BITE.   I'LL BITE.

(they look at each other – kismet)

...FOR HE'S SO MUCH
MORE
THAN JUST A GUY.

YES SHE LOVES THAT   YES I LOVE THAT
HE ISN'T

I'M ISN'T –

YOU MEAN YOU AREN'T –

YOU MEAN I'M NOT –

I MEAN

YOU MEAN
YOU LOVE THAT   I LOVE THAT
I'M NOT

YOU ISN'T

JUST A GUY!   JUST A GUY!
OOH-OOH-OOH...

PRINCESS. Mm, that's pretty.

FLEA. I know.

I like singing with you.

STORYTELLER. *(looking at the* **PROFESSOR***)* If only love were always so easy.

FLEA. Splendid woman, I must know your name!

PRINCESS. In my language I am called Gobble-Gobble.

FLEA. That's beautiful. I think I love you, Gobble-Gobble.

PRINCESS. You're not doing the "b"s right. Because there is only one word in our language, subtle shifts of tone and inflection are very important.

FLEA. Say it again.

PRINCESS. Gobble-Gobble.

FLEA. *(It sounds exactly like what she said.)* Gobble-Gobble.

PRINCESS. No. Gobble-Gobble.

FLEA. *(a little different)* Gobble-Gobble.

PRINCESS. 'Fraid not.

FLEA. *(a little more different)* Gobble-Gobble?

PRINCESS. Still wrong. But in your language, you may call me "Sally".

FLEA. Princess Sally. It is like sweetest birdsong!

PROFESSOR. This is all very moving, but what was that bit about eating us for dinner?

PRINCESS. You.

PROFESSOR. What?

PRINCESS. Not him. Just you.

(*She takes a threatening little bite out of the air.*)

(*There is a trumpet flourish, from a way's off.*)

FLEA. What was that?

PRINCESS. My parents are coming. Now they can meet you and we can eat your boring friend!

FLEA. Oh good!

PROFESSOR. What?

FLEA. I mean, you can't eat the Professor!

PRINCESS. And why not?

FLEA. Well, it wouldn't be right.

PRINCESS. Why not?

FLEA. *(to the* **PROFESSOR***)* She makes a strong case.

PROFESSOR. What?!

FLEA. Because he's my friend. And we don't eat our friends. We may drink their blood now and then, but we don't eat them.

PRINCESS. Why not.

FLEA. *(finally defiant)* Because if you eat him, you can't marry me.

PRINCESS. *(as if she doesn't know the word)* I…"can't?"

STORYTELLER. The Princess had never been told she couldn't do anything, ever.

(We hear the trumpet flourish, very close now.)

PROFESSOR. Oh no.

FLEA. Please, Princess Sally. Won't you help us?

STORYTELLER. And a strange thing happened. For the first time in her life, the Princess did something unselfish.

PRINCESS. Quick, we must hide your boring friend.

PROFESSOR. Where? *(remembering to be offended)* I mean "Hey!"

PRINCESS. Behind my Pretty Pink Flamingo Feather Fan! Hurry!

(She unfurls her lovely fan. The **PROFESSOR** *hides behind it, although it is much too small to conceal him.*

(Note: The lines in parentheses below are translations of the Cannibal language. The sense of these lines may be shamelessly overstated by the actors [e.g. Using a ring finger to indicate the word "marry"].)

(The **LOYAL SUBJECT** *enters, playing his trumpet flourish. The* **CANNIBAL KING** *enters.)*

CANNIBAL KING. *("Greetings, daughter" – ceremonious)* Gobble, Gobble!

(The **LOYAL SUBJECT** *plays a more intricate flourish. The* **CANNIBAL QUEEN** *enters.)*

CANNIBAL QUEEN. *("Greetings, daughter")* Gobble, Gobble!

PRINCESS. *("Hi father, Hi mother" – with a curtsey to each of them)* Gobble Gobble.
Gobble Gobble.

CANNIBAL QUEEN. *("Who is your new friend?")* Gobble Gobble Gobble?

PROFESSOR. *(aside to us)* What strange savage language is this?

PRINCESS . *("May I present, the fantastic flea!")* Gobble Gobble…Gobble!

FLEA. *(extending his hand)* Gobble Gobble.

CANNIBAL KING. *(to* **PRINCESS***)* Gobble?

PRINCESS. He said Gobble Gobble.

CANNIBAL KING. *(shaking the* **FLEA***'s hand now)* Ah, Gobble Gobble.

CANNIBAL QUEEN. *("Pleased to meet you")* Gobble gobble.

(The **FLEA** *kisses her hand.)*

STORYTELLER. *(fiddling with the switch on the wall)* This is very strange. The Cannibal Translator seems to be broken.

(The **CANNIBAL KING** *sniffs the air aggressively.)*

CANNIBAL KING. *("I could swear I smelled human")* Gobble Gobble human.

PRINCESS. *("Whatever do you mean, Father?")* Gobble Gobble, Gobble?

CANNIBAL KING. *("It's coming from over there")* Gobble gobble…

(The **CANNIBAL KING** *is getting close to the flamingo*

fan. The **PRINCESS** *and the* **FLEA** *try to block his way.*)

PRINCESS. (*"Daddy, don't be silly"*) Gobble, gobble gobble.

(*The* **PROFESSOR** *sneezes, his nose tickled by the pretty pink feathers.*)

CANNIBAL KING. (*"I thought I heard someone sneeze!"*) Gobble gobble "Choo!"

CANNIBAL QUEEN. (*"Lester, your heart"*) Gobble, gobble gobble.

(*The* **PROFESSOR** *sneezes again.*)

CANNIBAL KING. (*"There it was again!"*) Gobble! Gobble gobble "Choo!"

PRINCESS. (*"Oh, that's just part of the new pop song we're practicing!"*) "Choo!" Gobble gobble gobble new pop song!

(*The* **PRINCESS** *and the* **FLEA** *sing an infectious, Carnevale-inflected pop song to distract the* **CANNIBAL KING.** *The translation appears to the right.*)

(*SONG: GOBBLE*)

PRINCESS.

GOBBLE GOBBLE GOBBLE? CHOO.	(*Do you know how to dance? It's easy.*)
GOBBLE GOBBLE GOBBLE? CHOO!	(*Do you know? It's easy-breezy!*)
GOBBLE GOBBLE GOBBLE GOBBLE	(*Dance is the language*)
GOBBLE GOBBLE GOBBLE GOBBLE!	(*That everyone speaks!*)
CHOO! CHOO!	

(*The* **FLEA** *joins in, catching on.*)

PRINCESS & FLEA.

GOBBLE GOBBLE GOBBLE? CHOO.	(*Do you know how to dance? It's easy.*)
GOBBLE GOBBLE GOBBLE? CHOO!	(*Do you know? It's easy-breezy!*)

GOBBLE GOBBLE GOBBLE GOBBLE	*(Dance is the language)*
GOBBLE GOBBLE GOBBLE GOBBLE!	*(That everyone speaks!)*
GAWWWWWBLE,	*(Don't worry,)*
GOBBLEDY GAWWWWWBLE	*(Don't worry if you haven't had lessons.)*
GOBBLE GOBBLE GOBBLE? CHOO.	*(Come dance with me! It's easy.)*
GOBBLE GOBBLE GOBBLE? CHOO!	*(Come, I'll show you how!)*

(The **CANNIBAL KING** *joins in now, unable to resist the beat.)*

PRINCESS & FLEA & CANNIBAL KING.

GAWWWWWBLE,
GOBBLEDY GAWWWWWBLE.
GOBBLE GOBBLE GOBBLE? CHOO.
GOBBLE GOBBLE GOBBLE?

PRINCESS & FLEA & CANNIBAL KING & CANNIBAL QUEEN & LOYAL SUBJECT.

OOOOOOOH!
GOBBLE GOBBLE GOBBLE? CHOO.
GOBBLE GOBBLE GOBBLE? CHOO!
GOBBLE GOBBLE GOBBLE GOBBLE
GOBBLE GOBBLE GOBBLE GOBBLE!
CHOO! CHOO!

(The **PROFESSOR** *leaps from behind the fan and joins in. He can't help himself — the song is so infectious.)*

ALL.

GOBBLE GOBBLE GOBBLE? CHOO.
GOBBLE GOBBLE GOBBLE? CHOO!
GOBBLE GOBBLE GOBBLE GOBBLE GOBBLE

(big finale:)

GOBBLE GOBBLE GOBBLE GA-GA-GOBBLE-GA...
GOBBLE!

(The **PROFESSOR** *does a grand-finale gesture. Then he*

realizes he's revealed himself.)

PROFESSOR. Uh-oh.

CANNIBAL KING. *("So, there is a human! I knew it!")* Gobble. Gobble human gobble!

PRINCESS. *("Please Father, I'm in love!")* Gobble gobble, gobble gobble!

CANNIBAL KING. *("Not with this intruder?")* Gobble *gobble?*

PRINCESS. *("No, of course not...")* Gobble. Gobble gobble...

(*The* **STORYTELLER** *has been getting nowhere fiddling with the translator machine. Finally she pounds on it with her fist in frustration.)*

....gobble but if we eat him, I can never marry his friend the Flea!

CANNIBAL KING. You're too young to get married anyway.

STORYTELLER. Thank goodness! That was getting really annoying.

PRINCESS. I am not too young!

CANNIBAL KING. Twelve is too young! You're not even allowed to pierce your ears yet.

PRINCESS. I know, and it's so unfair.

CANNIBAL QUEEN. Most girls these days are getting married after college.

PRINCESS. I don't want to go to college.

CANNIBAL QUEEN. Oh Lord.

PRINCESS. I love him, and I'll wait as long as I have to!

FLEA. So will I.

PROFESSOR. Me too.

CANNIBAL KING. This doesn't concern you.

PROFESSOR. Doesn't concern me? I'm the one who's getting eaten!

CANNIBAL KING. That's right! For once I'm putting my foot down, Sally. The human will be sacrificed in the Cannibalia tomorrow!

PRINCESS. *(pouting, not a crisis)* Father, this is so unfair.

CANNIBAL KING. Take him away!

    (The **LOYAL SUBJECT** *leads the* **PROFESSOR** *off.)*

    (continuous into:)

VI. THE NEW KING OF THE CANNIBALS.

(The **CANNIBALS** *start hanging up party decorations, blowing up balloons, etc.)*

STORYTELLER. What, you may be wondering, is the Cannibalia?

Only the grandest day of the whole Cannibal year.

Imagine the best birthday party you ever went to. Well it's that times twelve.

It took them all day to put up the decorations and make the treats. Oh my goodness, the treats: There were cotton-candy canes, and chocolate-covered chocolates, and ice cream Fridays. Best of all, they added sugar to the sea water – so when you went swimming, you got a mouthful of sweet not salty.

Still, no party would be complete without…

CANNIBALS. Slow-cooked fancy human!

(The **CANNIBAL KING** *and the* **LOYAL SUBJECT** *wheel on the* **PROFESSOR**, *tied up in the cauldron now. The* **CANNIBAL QUEEN** *seasons him.)*

PROFESSOR. This is all rather humiliating.

CANNIBAL QUEEN. A pinch of salt…

A pinch of pepper…

(The **PROFESSOR** *sneezes.)*

God bless you.

And last of all, a pinch of paprika.

Wait a minute. I can't find the paprika.

I know it was around here somewhere…

CANNIBAL KING. We can't cook the human without paprika.

CANNIBAL QUEEN. *(a domestic moment)* Don't you think I know that?

PRINCESS. Psst!

(The **PRINCESS** *shows him a big jar labeled "Paprika".)*

FLEA. *(whispering to the* **PRINCESS***)* The paprika!

PRINCESS. That should keep them busy while we untie the Professor.

FLEA. Beautiful *and* clever!

CANNIBAL QUEEN. *(to* CANNIBAL KING, *taking out another big jar)* Luckily, I always keep an extra jar of paprika on hand.

FLEA & PRINCESS. Oh no!

PRINCESS. We have to stall somehow.

FLEA. Somehow *how?*

> *(The* CANNIBAL QUEEN *seasons the* PROFESSOR *with paprika.)*

CANNIBAL QUEEN. Perfect.

CANNIBAL KING. Just one more dash!

CANNIBAL QUEEN. *Two* dashes of paprika? That would be just decadent.

> *(The* STORYTELLER *coughs pointedly, in case we missed the Word of the Day.)*

FLEA. *(to the* PRINCESS*)* I have an idea.

PRINCESS. What?

FLEA. Mesdames et Messieurs, gather round!
I will now recite a poem by the inimitable John Donne.

CANNIBAL KING. What's inimitable mean?

CANNIBAL QUEEN. I think it means he tastes good.

FLEA. You're in for a real treat. I know all twenty-seven verses by heart. *(aside to the* PRINCESS:*)* While I entrance them with my dramatic skills, you can free the Professor.

CANNIBAL QUEEN. What was that?

PRINCESS. Nothing, Mother.

FLEA. *(extra-proper in tone)* Ah-ah-*hem.*
"Mark but this flea, and mark in this,
How little that which thou deniest me is[*];
It suck'd me first, and now sucks thee,

---

[*]Very important: He makes "is" rhyme with "this."

And in this flea our two bloods mingled be!"

(light shifts to the **PRINCESS** *trying to untie the* **PROFESSOR***)*

PRINCESS. *(with effort)* It's – too – tight!

PROFESSOR. Keep trying.

PRINCESS. Daddy is very good at knots. He was in the Cannibal Navy.

(Light shifts back to the **FLEA***. The* **CANNIBAL KING** *and* **CANNIBAL QUEEN** *have slumped a little lower in their seats now, their eyes heavy-lidded. The* **LOYAL SUBJECT** *is riveted.)*

FLEA. "O stay, three lives in one flea spare,
Where we almost, yea, more than married are.
This flea is you and I, and this
Our marriage bed, and marriage temple is!"

(Light shifts back to the **PRINCESS** *and the* **PROFESSOR***.)*

PRINCESS. It – won't – budge!

PROFESSOR. What verse is he on?

PRINCESS. Somewhere in the teens.

PROFESSOR. Hurry!

PRINCESS. Maybe I can eat through the knot.

(She starts to chew, as light shifts back to the **FLEA***'s performance. He is on the 27th and final verse. The* **CANNIBAL KING** *and* **CANNIBAL QUEEN** *have fallen asleep, but the* **LOYAL SUBJECT** *is deeply moved, dabbing his eyes with a handkerchief.)*

FLEA. "Cruel and sudden, hast thou since
Purpled thy nail in blood of innocence?
Wherein could this flea guilty be,
Except in that drop which it suck'd from thee?"

(The **FLEA** *curtseys deeply.)*

Thank you. Thank you.

(The **LOYAL SUBJECT** *nudges the* **CANNIBAL KING** *and* **CANNIBAL QUEEN** *awake. They start clapping reflexively.)*

LOYAL SUBJECT. Marvelous.

CANNIBAL KING. A triumph.

CANNIBAL QUEEN. I liked the part about drinking blood.

CANNIBAL KING. And now, at long, long last, we begin the slow cooking of the slow-cooked fancy human!

(They all look over at the cauldron. The **PRINCESS** *is still chewing through the last of the ropes.)*

CANNIBAL QUEEN. Sally?

PRINCESS. *(lisping)* Ow. I think I got a tongue splinter.

FLEA. Who's up for another poem?

CANNIBAL KING. *(to* **PRINCESS***)* You dare defy me!

CANNIBAL QUEEN. *(to* **CANNIBAL KING***)* Lester, calm down. Your heart…

CANNIBAL KING. For this, both intruders must die!

PRINCESS. *(still lisping)* Father, no! There has to be some way to make you spare them.

CANNIBAL KING. There is none!

LOYAL SUBJECT. There is one!

ALL. *(including* **STORYTELLER***)* What?

(Everyone turns to the **LOYAL SUBJECT***. He takes out a stone tablet. It is very very heavy.)*

LOYAL SUBJECT. It is written, in the ancient Code of Cannibal,
That whomsoever can make the King laugh will be crowned the new King of the Cannibals.

PROFESSOR. All we have to do is make him laugh?

FLEA. That shouldn't be too hard.

CANNIBAL QUEEN. He hasn't laughed for a hundred and two years.

FLEA. Uh-oh.

PROFESSOR. That *is* a long time.

But never underestimate the power…of tickling!

STORYTELLER. So they tickled him

And tickled him

And tickled him

And tickled him

(pause)

And tickled him

And tickled him

And tickled him

CANNIBAL KING. Hmmph.

STORYTELLER. …But the old King didn't even crack a smile.

PRINCESS. Tickle faster!

PROFESSOR. Tickle harder!

FLEA. I'm tickling as hard as I can!

CANNIBAL KING. Do your worst.

I shall not laugh, never ever!

PRINCESS. I have an idea.

STORYTELLER. And with that, the Princess took the single pinkest feather from her pretty pink flamingo fleather fan.

Pretty pink plamingo feather plan.

Flamingo pleather pan.

PRINCESS. *(impatiently plucking the feather)* Flamingo feather fan!

CANNIBAL KING. Oh no, oh no.

PRINCESS. *(handing the feather to the* **FLEA***)* Oh yes.

CANNIBAL KING. The Feather of Infinite Tickles! You wouldn't!

PRINCESS. We would.

I suggest you start with his foot.

(The **FLEA** *tickles the* **CANNIBAL KING***'s foot aggressively with the feather.)*

STORYTELLER. So the Flea tickled him
> And tickled him
> And tickled him
> And an astonishing thing happened...
> *(The tiniest hint of a giggle from the* **CANNIBAL KING.** *)*

STORYTELLER. *(cont.)* You'd barely notice it at first.
> You might think he was about to sneeze,
> Or wheeze,
> Or cough,
> Or scoff, but –

(The **CANNIBAL KING** *lets out a giant guffaw. He can't stop laughing.)*

PRINCESS. I knew it!

FLEA. Hooray!

PROFESSOR. Is he okay?

(The **CANNIBAL KING** *is rolling on the floor, laughing.)*

CANNIBAL QUEEN. He'll be like this for a while.
> He has a hundred-and-two years of laughing to catch up on.

FLEA. You're taking this rather well.

CANNIBAL QUEEN. *(with a shrug)* I've been trying to get him to lighten up for the last hundred-and-one years. I say Lester, you need a hobby – he never listens.

PROFESSOR. Princess, I owe you my life.

PRINCESS. Well, I'm sorry I called you boring and tried to eat you.

PROFESSOR. I'm sorry I called you a spoiled little brat.

PRINCESS. When was that?

PROFESSOR. Off stage.

(light shifts)

STORYTELLER. This year, Cannibalia began with the coronation of a new king.

PRINCESS. Here he comes!

(As the **FLEA** *is carried on in a sedan chair, the* **CANNIBALS** *sing the…)*

*(**SONG: CORONATION SONG**)*

(It starts as a solemn processional with much pomp and circumstance – think Charles and Di's wedding – before devolving into full party mayhem.)

CANNIBALS.
> HAIL TO THE KING
> MAY HE RULETH WITH EASE
> HAIL TO THE KING
> FOR HE IS THE BEES' KNEES!
> BRING OUT THE BLING,
> LOUD MAY WE SING:
> LONG LIVE THE KING,
> 'TIS A NEW ERA OF FLEAS!
> 'TIS A NEW ERA
> AND OUR KING'S THE BEES' KNEES!

PROFESSOR. *(to someone in the audience, a little desperate)* I knew him before he was famous.

(The **CANNIBALS** *bring the* **FLEA** *various things as they sing about them:)*

CANNIBALS.
> FIRST COMES THE SCEPTER, FOR POWER AND GRACE
> THEN COMES THE CROWN, USED FOR FRAMING HIS FACE!

(They throw rice.)

> NEXT, FOR GOOD LUCK, TOSS A HANDFUL OF RICE
> AND BRAND NEW CLEAN WHITE SOCKS, JUST BECAUSE THEY
> > SMELL NICE.

(They put a necklace of teeth on him.)

> SHARK'S TEETH, FOR COURAGE – NO WE CAN'T FORGET
> > THOSE
> AND ONLY THE KING WEARS A BONE THROUGH HIS NOSE!

FLEA. Hey –

LOYAL SUBJECT. *(attaching a bone to his nose)* Don't worry, it's a clip-on.

CANNIBALS.

BRING OUT HIS SWORD (MAY HE NEVER NEED TO USE IT)
AND THE KEY TO THE KINGDOM (HE BETTER NOT LOSE IT)
A CUPFUL OF SNAKE SPIT, IN OUR FAVORITE CUP
WHICH THE KING DRINKETH DOWN –

(The **FLEA** *looks into the cup, grossed out.)*

CANNIBALS.

YES HE DRINKS IT ALL DOWN –

(The **FLEA** *holds his nose, then drinks.)*

YES HE DRINKS IT ALL DOWN, AND IT CAN'T COME BACK UP!
AND ONCE ALL THESE THINGS HAVE BETOKENED HIS
    TROTH
THEN LAST BUT NOT LEAST
OUR NEW KING MUST TAKE
THE SACRED CANNIBAL OATH…

(Everyone looks on, expectant. The **FLEA** *reads from a stone tablet held by the* **LOYAL SUBJECT***:)*

FLEA.

LONG MAY I RULETH!
MAY MY RULETH BE COOLETH!
MAY IT NEVER BE CRUELETH!

PROFESSOR. *(jealous grumbling)* Highly questionable grammar.

(The **LOYAL SUBJECT** *blows a hot Latin lick on his trumpet, signaling the beginning of Cannibalia.)*

CANNIBALS.

TIME FOR CANNIBALIA!

(Another hot Latin lick. The tempo quickens, party mayhem ensues.)

CANNIBALIA!

CANNIBAL QUEEN.

WHEN THE SUN DIPS DOWN BELOW THE TREELINE
AND YOU HEAR THE TRUMPET CALL,
MOVE THE TABLES BACK, EVERYBODY MAKE A BEELINE
    FOR…

CANNIBALS.
> CANNIBALIA!

CANNIBAL QUEEN.
> FEEL THE PARTY BUBBLING UP
> FROM THE TOPS OF YOUR TOES
> SMELL THE SAVORY SWEETNESS
> WAFTING INSIDE OF YOUR NOSE
> IT'S A CHANCE TO BE CRAZY AND WILD BECAUSE
> ANYTHING...

CANNIBALS.
> ANYTHING GOES!
> CANNIBALIA!

(The **CANNIBALS** *dance the official dance of Cannibalia. It is wild and a bit strange. The* **FLEA** *gamely joins in, one step behind. They are impressed.)*

CANNIBALS.
> BRING OUT THE BLING
> LOUD MAY WE SING:
> LONG LIVE THE KING,
> 'TIS A NEW ERA OF FLEAS!
> 'TIS A NEW ERA
> AND OUR KING –
> HE'S THE BEES' KNEES!

STORYTELLER. All night the air was filled with song, and everyone was filled with happiness, and no one felt lonely.

(Lights on the **PROFESSOR.** *Music suddenly out.)*

Well, almost no one.

(The **PROFESSOR** *blows one of the noisemakers from the party, sadly. Like the sad whistle-blowing after Livia left.)*

Everything should have been fine – The Professor was given a fine cabana to live in, with walls made of sugar cane that you could lick all day long. And a fine hammock to sleep in, which reminded him of being back in his father's balloon. He could think of nothing else.

(The **PROFESSOR** *sings a wistful little reprise of* **UP UP UP***:)*

PROFESSOR.
UP, UP, UP IN THE SKY
THAT'S THE ONE PLACE, THE ONE PLACE TO BE
I CAN'T GET THERE MYSELF
BUT PERHAPS WITH A FLEA...

(The **FLEA** *sees this from a distance.)*

PROFESSOR.
UP, UP, UP IN THE SKY
THAT'S THE ONE PLACE, THE ONE PLACE TO GO
ALL THE TROUBLES OF MAN
SO FAR DOWN BELOW.

STORYTELLER. Sometimes, in the dead of night, the Professor thought he could see Livia in the light of the moon reflecting off the ocean.

PROFESSOR. Livia, is that you?

STORYTELLER. It's just your imagination.

PROFESSOR. I thought I heard you talking to someone.

STORYTELLER. *(almost busted)* Maybe you're imagining I'm here because you miss me.

PROFESSOR. I do. I do miss you.

(light shifts)

STORYTELLER. *(to us again)* The Flea lived in the cabana next door with the Princess. He liked to sit upon her delicate hand or her fair neck. She truly had changed, and was no longer heard to bully anyone –

PRINCESS. But *I* want to be the racecar!

STORYTELLER. ...Except, of course, when they played Monopoly.

FLEA. All right, my dear. Then I'll be the thimble.

PRINCESS. No, no – *you* be the racecar.

FLEA. Really?

PRINCESS. Really. I want you to have it.

STORYTELLER. She had learned that thinking of others is almost as fun as being selfish, and it's much better for the environment. What a delightful time the Princess was having, and the Flea too. But the Professor was not so delighted.

PROFESSOR. I am not so delighted.

STORYTELLER. He was a traveler at heart. And while he ate good food…

LOYAL SUBJECT. *(lifting the lid off a silver tray)* Fresh emu eggs, elephant eyes, and fried giraffe legs!

STORYTELLER. …he longed for the open road and the feeling of wind in his face. So the Professor did something he'd been dreaming of ever since his father disappeared beyond the clouds. He started to sew a balloon.

(The actors inflate an enormous life-sized balloon over the audience. I imagine that we're not looking at the balloon so much as we're all inside of it.)

What did he make the balloon out of, you ask? The Professor was very clever about it. He pretended that the hammock he slept in was uncomfortable.

LOYAL SUBJECT. What seems to be the trouble, Sir?

PROFESSOR. My back is very sensitive.

LOYAL SUBJECT. Very good, Sir. I'll see what I can do.

STORYTELLER. Every night he had a new hammock…

PROFESSOR. This just won't do.

LOYAL SUBJECT. Yes, Sir. Right away, Sir.

STORYTELLER. And every morning he complained again…

LOYAL SUBJECT. What now?

PROFESSOR. *(pushing at it with distaste)* I think it's broken.

STORYTELLER. …Until he had all the hammocks he needed for sewing an enormous balloon. But he still needed something to make it lighter than air.

PROFESSOR. I know!

STORYTELLER. Clever man, he collected the hydrogen gas emitted by the eruptions of the local volcano.

(The **PROFESSOR** *holds out an open mason jar, as there's a large quaking sound.)*

STORYTELLER. Now, if only he could find something to fill the sandbags with…

(The **PROFESSOR** *paces, looking down at the sand.)*

PROFESSOR. I could think better if it wasn't for all this sand.

STORYTELLER. *(hintingly)* He needed something to fill the *sand*bags with.

PROFESSOR. I've got it:
Sand!

VII. HOMEWARD BOUND.

STORYTELLER. The Cannibals all gathered on the beach to see the great balloon inflated. They watched as the hammocks twisted and hissed and came to life like a hungry beast. Only the strongest Cannibals could hold the ropes that kept the balloon on the ground. When it was all done, the balloon stretched over seven stories high. It was quite the tallest and most glorious thing any of the Cannibals had ever seen.

(Right about now, the balloon finishes "inflating." The final effect should be luminous and warm and exciting. In this special space, we hear the faint sound of wind whistling.)

CANNIBAL KING. Who ever saw such a thing?

CANNIBAL QUEEN. I'll get my camera!

CANNIBAL KING. Why do you always have to get that thing out?

PROFESSOR. Cannibal citizens, I can never thank you enough for your hospitality. And, while goodbyes are sad, I am excited for this chance to demonstrate the latest in aeronautical engineering.

FLEA. Professor, this can't really be goodbye.

PROFESSOR. *(vulnerable)* You could come with me. Remember when we promised to travel the sky together? *(he wiggles his pinky)* You could come with me and have even greater adventures.

PRINCESS. I will not permit it!

FLEA. I love you, Princess Sally, but I'm my own flea.

PRINCESS. You're not thinking of going with him?

FLEA. I'll come and visit whenever I can.

*(The **PRINCESS** turns her back to him. She seems to be trying to bottle her anger.)*

He's my friend, and I gave him my pinky-swear.

STORYTELLER. For a moment, they thought the Princess was going to eat them all, right then and there. But then she did the most selfless thing of all:

PRINCESS. *(turning back to him)* Quickly. Don't say goodbye.

STORYTELLER. She let the Flea go.

PRINCESS. Quickly. It will be easier that way.

FLEA. I'll come back for you. You're the loveliest princess I've ever seen.

PRINCESS. I'm the only princess you've ever seen.

FLEA. *(gallant as hell)* And I need never see another.

LOYAL SUBJECT. What about his kingly duties?

CANNIBAL KING. *(taking the crown off the **FLEA**'s head and putting it on his own)* I will be more than happy to fill in.

STORYTELLER. The second they were in the balloon, a fierce wind picked up.

*(The **STORYTELLER** turns on a hand-held fan. The **LOYAL SUBJECT** and the **CANNIBAL KING** hold onto ropes attached to the basket.)*

LOYAL SUBJECT. *(the rope taut now)* We can't hold her much longer, Professor!

CANNIBAL KING. I'm getting a rope burn!

STORYTELLER. And with one great gust, the balloon rose into the air, high above the clouds and far away from that savage land.

PROFESSOR. Goodbye! Goodbye!

*(We hear the music of **UP UP UP**, sounding more triumphant now, as the balloon rises into the rafters. The **FLEA** whistles the tune, sadly, as he peers over the edge of the basket.)*

Are you seasick again?

FLEA. Not seasick. Heartsick.

PROFESSOR. Don't be sad. You'll see her again soon.

FLEA. Did you ever see Livia again?

PROFESSOR. No. I suppose not.

FLEA. *(looking over the edge)* I think I can still see her, way down there.

She's still standing on the beach, waving goodbye.

PRINCESS. That's what you think!

(The PRINCESS *pops into view in the basket.)*

FLEA. Princess Sally! How did you get here?

PRINCESS. I stowed away.

PROFESSOR. This is highly irregular.

FLEA. I thought I might never see you again!

PRINCESS. You won't lose me that easy.

FLEA. You're not mad that I left you behind?

PRINCESS. But you didn't leave me behind. *(squeezing him very hard)* And now I'm *never* going to let you go.

FLEA. *(barely able to speak)* O rapture.

PROFESSOR. We're floating awfully close to the sea. We'll have to drop some sandbags, now that we're carrying the extra load.

CANNIBAL QUEEN. *(popping into view)* There's also me.

PRINCESS. Oh no, it's my *mother.*

CANNIBAL QUEEN. I couldn't let you go unsupervised. Besides, I could use a little adventure.

PRINCESS. *(on a sigh)* I suppose we should go back for Daddy.

PROFESSOR. We won't be going anywhere if we don't release more sandbags.

(The FLEA *releases sandbags.)*

We're still too heavy somehow.

(The STORYTELLER *pops into view.)*

STORYTELLER. Um, there's also me.

PROFESSOR. Livia! *(suspicious:)* Is this a flashback?

STORYTELLER. No.

PROFESSOR. Is it my imagination?

STORYTELLER. No, I'm really here.

PROFESSOR. Where have you been the last five years?

STORYTELLER. I've been following you around narrating your story. Haven't you noticed?

PROFESSOR. *(stammering)* Well, I – but I thought you were – I'm confused.

STORYTELLER. *(tender)* I know.

PROFESSOR. Does this mean you're coming back?

STORYTELLER. I used to think we were too different to be together.
But the more I followed you around and told your story, the more I started to think – if a Flea and a Professor aren't too different to be friends, or a Flea and a weird cannibal girl –

PRINCESS. Hey!

STORYTELLER. – then how hard can it be for us? *(beat)* What I'm trying to say is, I missed you too.

PROFESSOR. Hooray!

STORYTELLER. Just promise me one thing.

PROFESSOR. What's that?

STORYTELLER. I'll never have to wear that stupid sparkly outfit again.

PROFESSOR. I swear it.

STORYTELLER. Or get cut in half. Or hit with tomatoes.

PROFESSOR. That's three things. *(beat)* I swear, I swear. Oh Livia!

FLEA. We're still flying too low, Professor.

PROFESSOR. Okay, are there any more stowaways down there?

SEA CAPTAIN. *(popping up)* Just me.

FLEA. Oh my gosh, the Sea Captain. We forgot!

PROFESSOR. I'm confused. Who are you supposed to be anyway?
A Captain or a Cannibal?

LOYAL SUBJECT. They're both me. *(as the **SEA CAPTAIN** again:)* Such is the magic of the theater!

(The basket of the balloon is very crowded now.)

PROFESSOR. Release more sandbags.

FLEA. We've dropped all of the sandbags, Professor.

PROFESSOR. Impossible. We're still too heavy. *(beat)* Okay everyone, suck in your stomachs. Hopefully that will make us light enough to get back home.

(The **PROFESSOR** *sings the thinnest song of all:)*

(SONG: THINK THIN)

PROFESSOR.

YOU CAN SEE VERY PLAINLY
THE STATE THAT WE'RE IN:
THINK THIN.

*(***EVERYONE*** *sucks in their stomachs, holding their breath.)*

MAKE YOUR MIDDLE AS MINI
AS A MINNOW'S FIN:
THINK THIN.

(They all gasp for air, then suck in again. The gasps become a kind of percussion.)

WE'D BE FLOATING JUST FINE
IF WE WERE ALL A SIZE FOUR

(He looks sideways at the **FLEA.** *)*

BUT A FEW OF OUR CREW
ARE SIZE FORTY OR MORE.
SO, SUCK IT IN…

ALL.

THINK THIN!

(They gasp.)

PROFESSOR.

YOU CAN SEE THAT THIS BASKET
IS FILLED TO THE BRIM

STORYTELLER.

THINK SLIM!

(They gasp.)

SEA CAPTAIN.

JUST PRETEND THAT YOU'RE SPAGHETTI

PRINCESS.

OR THE WIDTH OF A BEAN

FLEA.

THINK LEAN!

(They gasp.)

ALL.

EVERY PASSENGER'S REQUIRED
TO DO ALL THAT HE CAN

CANNIBAL QUEEN.

I COULD TRY TO START A DIET
OR AN EXERCISE PLAN –

ALL.

NO! SUCK IT IN…

(They gasp.)

THINK THIN!

(They let it out.)

FLEA.

IT'S THE ONLY WAY TO WIN!

ALL.

THINK THIN!

(They gasp.)

CANNIBAL QUEEN.

GLUTTONY IS A SIN!

ALL.

THINK THIN!

(They gasp.)

LOYAL SUBJECT.

AND THEN YOU'LL BE THIN!

ALL.

THINK THIN!

(They gasp.)

PRINCESS. *(to* **LOYAL SUBJECT***)*
YOU CAN'T RHYME "THIN" WITH "THIN!"
ALL.
THINK THIN!
JUST BY SUCKING IT IN!

THINK THIN!
THINK THIN!
THINK THIN!
THINK THIN!
THINK!

(They gasp.)

THIN!

(Everyone collapses from lack of oxygen. Spent but triumphant.)

STORYTELLER. I don't know if it was good science, but somehow it worked:

Soon we were flying high above the Atlantic Ocean, the light bouncing off the waves and onto our big beautiful balloon. From up in our basket, the whales and the sailboats looked as small as fleas. We waved hello as they passed by.

ALL. Hello! Hello!

STORYTELLER. And so the Professor and the Flea kept on with their act, and I came along to tell their story. And the Cannibals played themselves, of course. It worked so well, in fact, that we kept performing right up to this very *[afternoon/morning/night]* in the city of *[whatever city we're in]*.

(She regards the **FLEA** *and the* **PROFESSOR.***)*

Now when they travel, it is *first*-class, not fourth. For they have a wonderful balloon to take them everywhere. They are classy folk now, oh, most respectable folk:

STORYTELLER.	**HANS CHRISTIAN ANDERSEN.**
The Flea	"The Flea and the Professor."

(Light rises on **HANS CHRISTIAN ANDERSEN**, *who is writing the last line of his story with a flourish.)*

(continuous into…)

VIII. EPILOGUE.

(The **STORYTELLER** *opens a trunk and lifts out a charming, tiny house with lights on in all the windows.)*

STORYTELLER. This is Hans Christian Andersen at his house in Denmark. Finishing the exact story you've been watching today.

(The actors come out with a table, a chair, and an oil lamp, assembling Andersen's garret very quickly before our eyes.)

I'd be a pretty bad Storyteller if I didn't tell you that this was the very last story written by the man who gave us "The Little Mermaid," and "The Ugly Duckling," and "The Emperor's New Clothes." *(to the actors:)* Hurry now. Chop chop! Denmark is a far cry from that other land where the sand is white-hot. In Denmark, everything is blue-cool. And the sun is so weak that people carry candles all day long.

(Andersen's candle has burned down almost to a stub. The sun is just rising. The **FLEA***, the* **PROFESSOR***, and the* **PRINCESS** *are all there with him, although he doesn't seem to see them.)*

(The **PROFESSOR** *turns Andersen's lamp a little brighter. The* **FLEA** *holds up a window for him to look out of. The* **PRINCESS** *sharpens his pencil.)*

HANS CHRISTIAN ANDERSEN. *(holding it up to survey his work)* "There was once a hot-air balloonist, and things went badly for him…"

STORYTELLER. It wasn't his most perfect story, but it was one of those he loved best.

That happens with people sometimes – they love things that are oddly shaped. Like a teddy bear with one eye, or a dog with three legs. *(looking at the* **PROFESSOR***.)* Or a Professor.

PRINCESS. He had written many tales of sad mermaids and sad tin soldiers.

FLEA. Of things that ache so much to become human, they don't realize they already are.

PROFESSOR. But by now his bones ached and his eyes were dry and he had grown tired of writing of sad things.

(**HANS CHRISTIAN ANDERSEN** *opens the window, and shouts out of it.*)

HANS CHRISTIAN ANDERSEN. I am tired of writing of sad things!

STORYTELLER. …He was often heard to say, when the townspeople passed by.

So this time, he wrote a story about people who start out alone and end up, well,

PROFESSOR. *(tender, to the* **STORYTELLER***)* Not alone.

STORYTELLER. People who go off and make their way in the world. And a funny thing – Once he had written the story, the more he started to wonder:

HANS CHRISTIAN ANDERSEN. What's outside that window?

STORYTELLER. There had to be more than what he could see from his house.

(*The* **FLEA**, *the* **PRINCESS**, *the* **PROFESSOR**, *and the* **STORYTELLER** *watch him.*)

HANS CHRISTIAN ANDERSEN. There has to be sunlight, and Christmas, and crumpets; and how long you can keep from stepping on the cracks in the sidewalk.

FLEA. There have to be green M&M's.

PRINCESS. And letting people be the racecar.

PROFESSOR. And hot-air balloons that skim the top of the sky.

(*The door of the theater opens. Light pours in.*)

STORYTELLER. So, the great storyteller put down his pen and walked into the welcoming day.

(The cast waves goodbye to **HANS CHRISTIAN ANDERSEN** *as he exits through the open doors of the theater.)*

STORYTELLER. *(to the audience)* Now you do the same. I'm serious!

(The **STORYTELLER** *and the rest of the cast sing…)*

(SONG: THE GRAND FINALE)

STORYTELLER.
THE SHOW IS REALLY OVER
WE'VE NO MORE TALE TO TELL
NO PLOT POINT LEFT TO COVER

(selling it)

NO MORE BRASSY SONG TO SELL.

PROFESSOR.
IT'S THE END OF OUR PLAY
TIME TO TURN UP THE LIGHTS
PUT OUR COSTUMES AWAY
LOSE THE MAKE-UP.

FLEA & PRINCESS.
SO GET READY TO CLAP
WE'RE ON THE VERY LAST PAGE
IF YOU'RE TAKING A NAP,
TIME TO WAKE UP!

ALL.
THE SHOW IS TRULY OVER
WE REALLY MEAN IT NOW
HANS CHRISTIAN ANDERSEN HAS LEFT THE BUILDING
BUT WE JUST CAN'T
TAKE A BOW.
(They all join hands to bow but find that they can't quite do it.)
THE SHOW IS REALLY OVER

STORYTELLER.
FINITO, END OF SCENE.

PROFESSOR. *(performing a magic trick)*
> THERE'S NO MORE FEATS OF MAGIC

PRINCESS. *(doing a dance step)*
> NO MORE STEPS IN OUR ROUTINE!

FLEA.
> WE SHOULD GET ON WITH OUR DAY

CANNIBAL QUEEN.
> THERE'S A WORLD TO EXPLORE

SEA CAPTAIN/LOYAL SUBJECT.
> SHOULDN'T DAWDLE, DELAY, OR DILLY-DALLY

FLEA, PROFESSOR, STORYTELLER.
> BUT WE LIKE IT ON STAGE

PRINCESS, CANNIBAL QUEEN, LOYAL SUBJECT.
> SPENDING TIME WITH OUR FRIENDS

ALL.
> AND WE CAN'T SEEM TO QUIT
> THIS FINALE!
>
> THE SHOW IS TRULY OVER
> WE REALLY MEAN IT NOW
> I KNOW WE WERE HAVING SUCH A GOOD TIME
>
> *(gathering momentum)*
>
> BUT THERE'S NO CAUSE TO HESITATE
> BECAUSE THE NEXT STEP COULD BE GREAT
> IF WE B –
>
> *(They almost bow, but then stop at the last minute.)*
>
> THE WORLD OUTSIDE IS FUNNY AND FINE
> GO CHEW IT WITH YOUR MANDIBLES
> NOW GET YOUR COATS AND HATS AND THINGS
> (PLEASE DON'T FORGET YOUR VALUABLES)
> OH-OH-OH-OH-OH!
> THE SHOW IS REALLY OVER!
>
> *(another almost-bow)*
>
> THE SHOW IS ABSOTIVELY OVER!

(again)

ALL. *(cont.)*

THE SHOW IS POSILUTELY OVER!

(again)

WE'RE FINISHED! THE END – AND HOW!
WE'RE SO GLAD THAT YOU JOINED US
OH LOOK! HERE COMES THE BOW!

(They finally bow.)

End of Play